Dear Parent:
Your child's love of read

Every child learns to read in a different way and at his or her own speed. Some go back and forth between reading levels and read favorite books again and again. Others read through each level in order. You can help your young reader improve and become more confident by encouraging his or her own interests and abilities. From books your child reads with you to the first books he or she reads alone, there are I Can Read Books for every stage of reading:

SHARED READING
Basic language, word repetition, and whimsical illustrations, ideal for sharing with your emergent reader

BEGINNING READING
Short sentences, familiar words, and simple concepts for children eager to read on their own

READING WITH HELP
Engaging stories, longer sentences, and language play for developing readers

READING ALONE
Complex plots, challenging vocabulary, and high-interest topics for the independent reader

I Can Read Books have introduced children to the joy of reading since 1957. Featuring award-winning authors and illustrators and a fabulous cast of beloved characters, I Can Read Books set the standard for beginning readers.

A lifetime of discovery begins with the magical words **"I Can Read!"**

Visit www.icanread.com for information
on enriching your child's reading experience.

I Can Read® and I Can Read Book® are trademarks of HarperCollins Publishers.

The Bad Seed Goes to the Library
Text copyright © 2022 by Jory John
Illustrations copyright © 2022 by Pete Oswald
Interior illustrations by Saba Joshaghani in the style of Pete Oswald
All rights reserved. Printed in the United States of America.
No part of this book may be used or reproduced in any manner whatsoever without written permission except
in the case of brief quotations embodied in critical articles and reviews. For information address HarperCollins
Children's Books, a division of HarperCollins Publishers, 195 Broadway, New York, NY 10007.
www.icanread.com

Library of Congress Control Number: 2021945762
ISBN 978-0-06-295455-8 (pbk.)
ISBN 978-0-06-295456-5 (trade bdg.)

The artist used pencil sketches scanned and painted in Adobe Photoshop
to create the digital illustrations for this book.
22 23 24 25 26 LSCC 10 9 8 7 6 5 4 3 2 1
❖
First Edition

THE BAD SEED
Goes to the Library

Written by **JORY JOHN** • Cover illustration by **PETE OSWALD**

Interior illustrations by Saba Joshaghani
based on artwork by Pete Oswald

HARPER

An Imprint of HarperCollinsPublishers

I may be a bad seed

but I'm in a good mood.

Want to know why?

Because I'm at the library.

It's my favorite place on earth.

Oh yeah, it's true!

The library has incredible books.

It has nice librarians.

It has comfortable places to sit
and big windows, too.

Sure, I might accidentally
use my "outside voice" at first,
BUT HEY, THAT'S ALL
PART OF THE FUN!

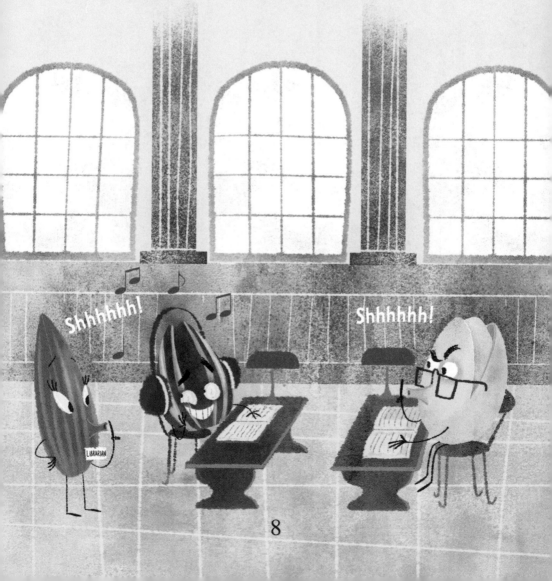

Anyway, I wonder
which book I'll choose.
The shelves are packed
with lots of great things to read.

9

Hmm. This one looks good.

And so does this.

And so does this.

Hmmmmmmm.

LOOK! I found a book!

It seems perfect for me.

It's called *The Speedy Seed*.

Now I'm going to find
a lovely reading spot.
Hmm.

Ahhhhhhhhhhhh! Yes.

This is the spot.

This is just right.

It's time to read.

Well, that was simply the best book
I've ever read in my life!
An instant classic.
I'm so glad that it's mine now.
I'm keeping it forever.
I'm going to read it over and over
and over again.

WHOOSH!

Hmm. A letter from the library?

Whoa! It says that my book is due.

Somebody else is waiting

to check out *The Speedy Seed*.

16

Who? What? WHY?

Excuse me? How dare they!

This book is mine!

Mine mine mine mine MINE!

Yes, this is my book
and I'm keeping it forever
and ever and ever.

The Speedy Seed

is so important to me.

I don't know what I would do

without it.

I think I'd feel bad. Really baaaad.

I guess it makes sense

that the library wants its book back.

Sigh.

But will anybody ever
enjoy this book as much as I do?

HUH? WILL THEY?!
I just don't know what to do!

21

I suppose it's important to share
good books with other seeds.

Because seeds who read
are smart, indeed.

But is there even another
book worth reading?
What if there isn't?

I guess I should go find out.
Yes, I'm off to the library again!

Hello, library.

Hello, new books.

Hello, comfy chairs.

Sheesh. It's time to return
The Speedy Seed.
At least I can borrow it again
some other day.

Here's the fellow who wants
The Speedy Seed.
He's been waiting to read it.

Boy oh boy is he excited.
I've made him so happy.

I'm a hero. Just like the Speedy Seed.

Now I can read something new.

Maybe I'll find something I like

as much as I liked that last book.

Maybe I won't.

But hey, that's the adventure

of reading.

I can read this.

Or this.

Or that.

Or this.

Or these.

Or those.

I wonder what I'll pick!

The possibilities are endless!

Gosh, this is my new favorite book.

Oh yeah, it's true!

I hope they NEVER

want it back!

30

Hmm.

A letter from the library?

I wonder what they want . . .

Oh no. No, no, no.

NOT AGAIN!

OH NOOOOOOOOOOOO!